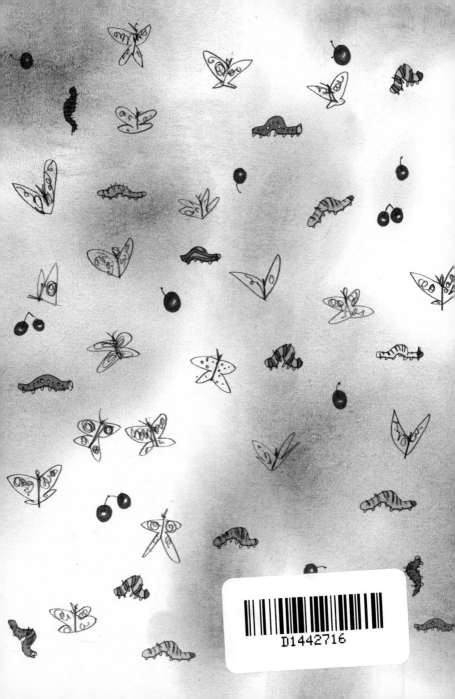

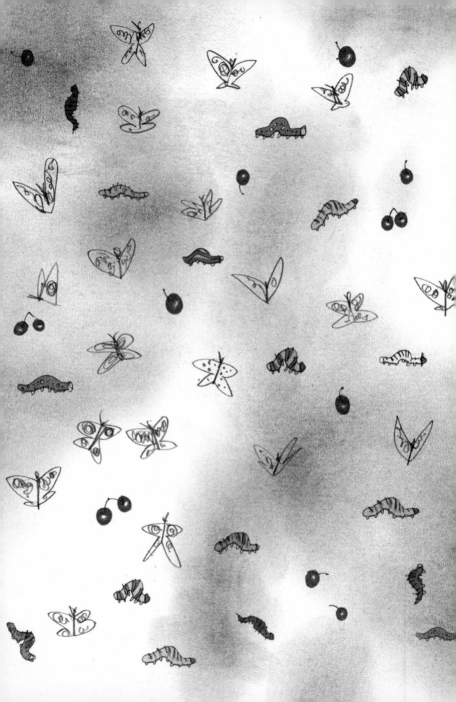

Mr Gum
and the
Cherry Tree

Shabba me whiskers! Andy Stanton's *Mr Gum* is winner of the Roald Dahl Funny Prize, the Red House Children's Book Award AND the Blue Peter Book Award for The Most Fun Story With Pictures. AND he's been shortlisted for LOADS of other prizes too! It's barking bonkers!

PRAISE FOR *Mr Gum*:

'Do not even think about buying another book – This is gut-spillingly funny.' Alex, aged 13

'It's hilarious, it's brilliant... Stanton's the Guv'nor, The Boss.' Danny Baker, BBC London Radio

'Funniest book I have ever and will ever read... When I read this to my mum she burst out laughing and nearly wet herself ... When I had finished the book I wanted to read it all over again it was so good.' Bryony, aged 8

'Funny? You bet.' Guardian

'Andy Stanton accumulates silliness and jokes in an irresistible, laughter-inducing romp.' Sunday Times

'Raucous, revoltingly rambunctious and nose-snortingly funny.' Daily Mail

'David Tazzyman's illustrations match the irreverent sparks of word wizardry with slapdash delight.' Junior Education

'This is weird, wacky and one in a million.' Primary Times

'It provoked long and painful belly laughs from my daughter, who is eight.' Daily Telegraph

'As always, Stanton has a ball with dialogue, detail and devilish plot twists.' Scotsman

'We laughed so much it hurt.' Sophie, aged 9

'You will laugh so much you'll ache in places you didn't know you had.' First News

'A riotous read.' Sunday Express

'It's utterly bonkers and then a bit more – you'll love every madcap moment.' TBK Magazine

'Chaotically crazy.' Jewish Chronicle

'Designed to tickle young funny bones.' Glasgow Herald

'A complete joy to read whatever your age.' This is Kids' Stuff

'The truth is a lemon meringue!' Friday O'Leary

'They are brilliant.' Zoe Ball, Radio 2

'Smooky palooki! This book is well brilliant.' Jeremy Strong

For Sandy
W'eeeeeey!
Well out of order!
Eggs!

EGMONT
We bring stories to life

Mr Gum and the Cherry Tree
First published 2010 by Egmont UK Limited, 239 Kensington High Street London W8 6SA

Text copyright © 2010 Andy Stanton
Illustration copyright © 2010 David Tazzyman

The moral rights of the author and illustrator have been asserted

ISBN 978 1 4052 5218 8

5 7 9 10 8 6

www.egmont.co.uk/mrgum

A CIP catalogue record for this title is available from the British Library

Printed and bound in Great Britain by the CPI Group

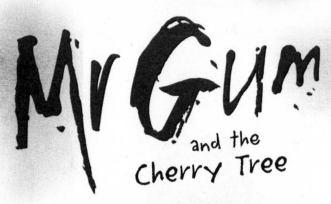

Mr Gum

and the
Cherry Tree

Andy Stanton

Illustrated by
David Tazzyman

EGMONT

Contents

Some of the crazy old townsfolk from Lamonic Bibber

Mrs Lovely

Friday O'Leary

Billy William the Third

Old Granny

Mr Gum

Martin Launderette

Alan Taylor

Polly

A grove there stands, where Runtus once did rule

High up above the world, 'mongst leafy bower;

And capering and singing, played the fool

And thus passed many a happy, blissful hour.

But fate may strip a King of all his power

And crown a fool a King in one fell blow;

And 'neath the petals of the fairest flower

Lieth poison in the darkness down below.

So to that grove, wise trav'ller, do not go.

– From *A Gentle Pilgrimme's Gyde to Lamonic Bibber,* 1581

Rough translation:

There was once a strange little bloke called Runtus who used to live in the forest. But things aren't always what they seem – so keep away or it might muck you up.

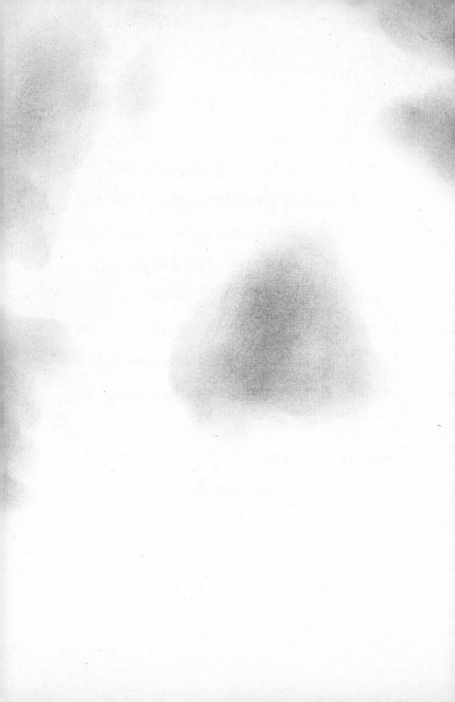

Chapter 1

Spring Fever

Yes! No! Maybe? What! Hello.

The whole squeak-mantling mess began on a day so innocent, a day so sweet and pure, a day so splendid, superb and smagnificent it could only be the first day of Spring. Ah, Spring!

Or as it is called in France, 'Le Boing'. It is a brilliant season, definitely in the top five.

And what a freshial, special Spring morning it was in the town of Lamonic Bibber, my friends! The sun was shining, the birds were playing Quidditch in the treetops and the ground was sort of just laying there letting people walk all over it. It was a glorious, give-me-morious, start-of-the-storious sort of a Spring morning. And as you can imagine with your tiny little brains, everyone was looking forward to it like a rascal.

'I'm looking forward to it like a rascal,' said Jonathan Ripples, the fattest man in town. 'I think I'll celebrate by eating not one, not two, but eight hot cross buns.'

'I'm looking forward to it like a rascal,' said Martin Launderette, who ran the launderette. 'I think I'll celebrate by spitting on not one, not two, but all eight of Jonathan Ripples' hot cross buns.'

'The old ways

'I'm looking forward to it like a rascal,' said a little girl called Peter. 'I think I'll read my favourite children's book – "Biffy the Worm Gets Arrested for Accidentally Murdering Everyone in canada". It's unputdownable!'

But just as everyone was about to settle down into their beautiful Spring mornings of eating, spitting and reading, a terrible shrieking was heard. It was Old Granny, the oldest woman in Lamonic Bibber. She was running up the high street and

are back!'

she was shrieking
at the top of
her voice.

'The Old
Ways are back!'
cried Old Granny as
she hinged it up the
street, her petticoats
all a-billow. 'The Old
Ways are back!'

'Oh, dear,' said Jonathan Ripples, shaking his big fat head big fat sadly. 'She's been at the sherry again.'

'LIES!' protested Old Granny, taking a quick sip of sherry from the bottle she always kept hidden in her handbag. 'I never touch the stuff! But listen! The Old Ways are back, I tell you!'

Well, by now quite a large crowd had gathered, and amongst them were two heroes you may know quite well. One was Friday O'Leary, a marvellous old fellow who knew the secrets of time and space. And the other was Polly, the happiest nine-year-old you could ever hope to meet. She was brave and true, like a how-do-you-do and she had everything she needed in life – a face, a couple of elbows and a pocket full of felt-tip pens. And hardly any of them had even run out.

'THE TRUTH IS A LEMON MERINGUE!' shouted Friday O'Leary, as he sometimes liked to do. 'What's all this then?'

'Shh,' said Polly. 'Old Granny's 'bout to speak.'

The townsfolk fell silent as Old Granny regarded them with a mysterious gaze. Then she fell asleep. Then she woke up and regarded them with another mysterious gaze. Then she fell asleep again.

'Told you she was drunk,' whispered Jonathan Ripples.

'LIES!' cried Old Granny, her eyes flying open into her most mysterious gaze yet. 'Now, here is my incredible news. The Old Ways have come back from before the days of Science! Ancient spirits have awoken! Strange wisps and fancies are amongst us! 'Tis the truth, 'tis the truth, 'tis the truth I tell, now come with me and I will show you well!'

'Ooooh,' went the little girl called Peter.

'Aaaah,' went Jonathan Ripples.

'CHIRP!' went Crazy Barry Fungus, who thought he was a chaffinch.

'The Old Ways are back!' cried the crowd – and they all set off after Old Granny, chanting for all they were worth.

🔊 🔊 🔊

'What does you reckons, Frides?' said Polly. 'Shall we follow them?'

'I think we'd better,' replied Friday, stroking his toes thoughtfully. 'They all seem to have gone a bit mad, and that is what is called "Spring Fever". Or as it is known in France, "Les Crazies de la Brains de la Boing-Boing".'

Chapter 2

Off to the Forest

*U*p at the top of Boaster's Hill, where the air is fresh and clean, and it's a lovely place to fly a kite and the stars come out and twinkle at night and I once saw a tramp there having a fight, with a cat dressed up as the Queen – yes, up at the top of Boaster's Hill, a school lesson was taking

place in the bright morning sunshine. And who was giving that lesson but Alan Taylor, the tiny gingerbread headmaster.

' . . . So as I have just demonstrated, children,' he was saying now, 'grass is very nice to sit on, but be careful because it can tickle. Now, can anyone tell me the name of this handsome creature over here?'

'Is it a rhino, sir?' said a girl called Caroline.

'Very close, Caroline,' said Alan Taylor kindly.

'Actually it is known as an "ant". Now, who can tell me –'

But just then there was an almighty ruckus and a rickus and a buckus and a bickus as over the hill came the crowd of townsfolk, with Old Granny leading the way. And each and every one of those townsfolk – whether young or old, rich or poor, tall or short, thin or Jonathan Ripples – each and every one of them was chanting 'The Old Ways are back! The Old Ways are back!'

'The old ways are back!'

'Hoi! What's going on?!' demanded Alan Taylor as the crowd stampeded through his lesson, scattering children and daisies in all directions. 'What's the meaning of this?'

'They all done gone mad with the Spring Fevers, Alan Taylor!' said Polly, rushing up with Friday O'Leary at her side. 'They're followin' Old Granny into adventures unknown!'

'Then we must follow them and keep them from harm!' said Alan Taylor. 'For they are but simple folk with simple legs and who knows what peril those legs could be marching them into? Children – get in line, single file!'

'Alan Taylor, you gots that class so well-behaved it's a marvel,' said Polly, as the schoolchildren jumped into formation.

'Yes,' replied the gingerbread headmaster, blowing on his silver Teaching Whistle to start the children marching in time. 'And when I think they used to be rowdy little goblins who loved

misbehaving and pinching each other, it makes me especially proud. I have tamed them,' he proclaimed, 'through the power of education and sometimes blowing a whistle at them.'

And so it went. Old Granny marched on. And the crowd of townsfolk marched behind her. And Polly and her friends marched behind them. And the schoolchildren marched behind *them*. Yes, there was certainly a lot of marching going on that morning, and actually it was even the month of March, so that counts as another one, kind of.

Onwards, onwards they marched. Over the fields and far away they marched. Up hill and down dale they marched. Over a glistening lake they marched –

'How did we march over a lake?' said Friday.

But somehow they just did, it was that sort of a day. Until eventually the crowd disappeared into a thick clump of trees.

'THE TRUTH IS A LEMON MERINGUE!' whispered Friday at the top of his voice. 'Look – Old Granny's leading them into the Forest of Runtus. Where the trees grow thick and plenty and they say ancient spirits do dwell.'

'Well, there's no goin' back now,' said Polly.

And so, Friday uttered the traditional words for entering forests that are said in that part of the world:

'Boo! Boo! Flappy flappy!
Boo! Boo! Flappy flappy!'

And they entered the Forest of Runtus.

the FOREST
of RUNTUS

'Ooh,' said the schoolchildren, 'it's scary in here.'

'That's because of the ancient spirits,' whispered Friday. 'This place is full of them. Enormous phantoms as small as your finger! And a phone that rings and when you answer it's ghosts! And a witch who lives in a pine cone and –'

Alan Taylor blew his silver Teaching Whistle sharply. 'Settle down, children,' he said.

'And enough of your tall tales, Friday. It's only a forest.'

But even so, it was a pretty spooky place. The only sounds were the rustling of the leaves and the soft sighing of the wind. The glooming trees crowded all around, making Polly shiver and Friday's hat whimper in fear. And the schoolchildren clutched at each other, half in terror and half in glee as they remembered Friday's stories of ancient spirits and forest folk.

Deeper they went into that forest, listening to the sounds. The sounds of the forest.

Whoooooosh.

Swiiiiishhhhhh.

SOOOOounnnds.

The woodpeckers pecked and the wouldn'tpeckers didn't. A ladybird sang a mournful song on her guitar. A dandelion chased a dandezebra through the undergrowth. And the path before them twisted and turned through the haunting trees like some sort of big curly super-finger, beckoning, beckoning them on.

At last they rounded a bend and came to an archway formed by two low branches. Two low branches all covered in roses. And beneath those curving branches stood Old Granny and her crowd, as solemn as calculators.

'Here we are,' whispered Old Granny, and the leaves and trees seemed to whisper it back –

Here we are, here we are, here we are . . .

'Our journey is at an end,' she whispered, and the leaves and trees seemed to whisper it back –

At an end, at an end, at an end . . .

'My leg hurts,' complained Martin Launderette, and the leaves and trees seemed to whisper it back –

Stop complaining, stop complaining, stop complaining. No one cares about your stupid leg, you cry-baby, cry-baby, cry-baby . . .

'This is where it all happened,' said Old Granny, once the leaves and trees had shut up. 'This is where I heard him.'

'Heard who?' asked the little girl called Peter.

But Old Granny had already ducked through the flowery archway. 'Follow me,' she cried. 'Follow me and see for yourselves!'

Chapter 3

Who Went Through the Arch?

ere's who went through the arch that morning:

First was Old Granny, then Martin Launderette, then the little girl called Peter,

a little boy called Rita and a baby called Elsie Wa-Wa. Then a really, really tall bloke called Harry Extreemoleg, then Thora Gruntwinkle with Greasy Ian and their pet monkey Philip the Horror, and then Jonathan Ripples, who got stuck in the archway and had to quickly go on a diet for ten minutes until he'd lost enough weight to squeeze through. Then came David Casserole (the Town Mayor), followed by Charlotte Casserole (his beautiful wife) and Frank Casserole (his beautiful husband). Next was Beany McLeany, wearing a bikini and reading a magaziney. After him came Pamela, Pamela, Pamela, Pamela, Pamela, Pamela, Pamela, Pamela, Pamela and Pamela – or 'The Pamelas' as they were known for short. Then came another Pamela who didn't count with the other Pamelas, because none of them liked her.

Then came a superhero called the Yellow Wriggler, who caught criminals by crawling along the ground dressed as a banana and shouting at them. After him came an illusionist called the **Prince of Illusions**. And after him came the **Prince of Illusions** again.

'Ha ha!' said the **Prince of Illusions**. 'The first time I went through the arch it was just an **ILLUSION**!'

Then came a few other people I can't be bothered to tell you about, then a couple more and then a couple more. And after them came the heroes – Polly, Friday and Alan Taylor, along with his class of giggling schoolchildren.

And finally came Crazy Barry Fungus,

tweet

tweet

hopping along in his silver birdcage and tweeting like a chaffinch. 'Tweet! Tweet!' said Barry Fungus. 'Tweet! Tweet! Wait for me! Wait for me!'

Chapter 4

Who Didn't Go Through the Arch?

Everyone else in the world.

And also the **Prince of Illusions**.

'Ha ha!' said the **Prince of Illusions**. 'The second time I went through the arch it was just another **ILLVSION**! I haven't gone through the arch at all and I never will. Goodbye!'

Chapter 5

The Voice in the Tree

'Ooooh,' said everyone as they stepped through the arch. 'This is nice!'

'See?' said Old Granny, pointing around the place and having a crafty sip of sherry while no one was looking. 'Told you it'd be good.'

And it was. Old Granny had led the townsfolk

to a forest clearing, which is like the rest of the forest only not quite so stuffed with trees.

'It's beautiful,' said Jonathan Ripples.

'It's wonderful,' breathed the little girl called Peter.

'Oh, what fair enchanted grove be this, where Time hath stood still for many hundreds of years and man hath seldom roamed?' marvelled one of The Pamelas. Not Pamela or Pamela or Pamela or Pamela or Pamela or Pamela or Pamela or Pamela or Pamela – but Pamela.

And indeed the air did feel magical. It was easy to believe the Old Ways were still at work in that place.

The grass waved softly in the breeze like the hair of long-ago princesses. A sparkling blue stream burbled and tinkled over moss-covered rocks as if to say,

'If you get thirsty I'll be there for you,

With my sparkling waters so wild and true.

But if you would drink from me, here is my warning

– A fish did a wee in me only this morning.'

An ancient stone statue of a goat stood crookedly in the grass, half grown over with ivy and hazelweed. And there was a bush, not just a bush but a nice bush.

But by far the biggest fatso in that clearing was the cherry tree. It was a shining, flaming phoenix amongst cherry trees! Its sturdy trunk reached proudly for the heavens. Its branches flung themselves far and wide like a rejoicing priest who's just discovered God hiding in his garage. And amongst its rich green leaves dangled hundreds of plump red cherries, fat and ripe and bursting with juicy secrets.

'Yes,' Old Granny told the mesmerised townsfolk. 'This is where it all happened. This is where I heard him.'

But even as she spoke, a strange voice suddenly rasped out of nowhere, shattering the day's calm like a rusty trampoline and shaking every single leaf in that place.

'WELL DONE, YOU STINKY OLD WOMAN,' said the voice. 'YOU'VE LED 'EM HERE, LIKE I COMMANDED.'

'It's him!' cried Old Granny, falling to her knees at the base of the tree and wrapping her arms around its trunk. 'Oh, great one! I would do anything for you!' And suddenly the townsfolk realised something amazing.

'That voice is coming from the cherry tree itself!' exclaimed Jonathan Ripples.

'It's true!' cried the little girl called Peter.

'Exactly!' said Old Granny triumphantly. 'That's what I've been saying all along – the Old Ways are back!'

'THAT'S RIGHT,' said the voice. And the leaves on the cherry tree rustled excitedly. 'COS GUESS WHO I FLIPPIN' WELL AM?'

'Batman?' said Friday.

'NO, YOU IDIOT,' growled the voice. And the leaves and the branches of the cherry tree shook even more wildly. 'HA HA HA! I AM THE MIGHTY **RUNTUS**, KING OF THE WOODLAND SPIRITS! I COME BACK FROM THEM OLDEN DAYS WHAT'S LOST IN THE MISTS OF TIME! I COME BACK TO RULE OVER YOU ALL!'

'Oh, great Runtus,' cried the crowd, dropping to their knees on the sacred earth around that fabulous tree. 'We have heard of you in legend and rhyme! Tell us how we may serve you, oh great one!'

'RIGHT!' yelled the voice. 'FIRST UP, I'M ABSOLUTELY STARVIN'! YOU THERE! THE BIG FAT ONE! GO AN' GET ME SOME SNACKS, TUBS!'

'Yes, oh great Runtus,' said Jonathan Ripples, almost falling over his own stomach in his haste.

'AND YOU – YOU STUPID MAYOR!' said the voice. 'GIMME THEM EXPENSIVE SHOES WHAT YOU'RE WEARIN'!'

'Yes, oh great Runtus,' said David Casserole, pulling off his Italian loafers and flinging them into the tree.

'AND YOU – THE LITTLE BOY WITH THE UGLY FACE! GO AN' FIND ME A –'

But Polly had had enough.

'Holds on just one minute,' she said, stepping into the centre of the clearing. 'Townsfolk, are you really gonna fall for this? I'll bets you all the money in the world PLUS some transfers what I got free with a comic – I'll bets you ANYTHIN' it's Mr Gum in that tree!'

'Mr Gum?' murmured the crowd in dismay. 'What, that old horror?'

'Yeah,' said Polly. 'Mr Gum. With his nasty old beard an' his fierce old eyes an' his hat what hardly even fits on his pointy old head!'

'SHUT UP, YOU MEDDLIN' LITTLE GIRL!' shouted the voice in the tree. 'I'M DEFINITELY RUNTUS – AN' WHAT'S MORE I CAN PROVE IT. OI, BILL! GET OUT HERE, ME OLD PAL FROM THE OLDEN DAYS!'

And then there came a rustling in the bushes, and the crowd gasped as out popped something they had never seen, but had only heard about in the legends of old. It was an amazing beast with the head of a man – and the body of a stinking great horse. 'Neeeigh!' said the strange creature. 'Neeeeigh! Me name's Galloping Bill an' I'm a flippin' centaur from the Olden Days. Neeeeeeigh! Neeeeeigh! Neeeeeeigh! Neeeeeigh! Neeeeigh! Neeeeeeigh! Neeeeeeigh! Neeeeeeigh!'

'OI, GALLOPIN' BILL!' said the voice in the tree. 'STOP YER NEIGHIN' AN' GET ON WITH IT OR I'LL KICK YER BLIMMIN' TAIL OFF!'

'Oh, yeah, sorry, Runtus,' said Galloping Bill. 'Now, listen up, you lot,' he told the astonished townsfolk. 'Back in them Olden Days when Runtus ruled, it was brilliant. Everyone jus' lazed around eatin' cherries all day. There wasn't no work, there wasn't no school, there wasn't nothin' borin' at all. It was just cherries an' lazin', I tell ya!'

'HOORAY!' said the crowd.

'An' now yer luck's in!' continued the amazing centaur. 'Cos Runtus is back to make them Olden Days happen again!'

'HOORAY!' said the crowd.

'See you later!' said Galloping Bill. 'Neeeeeigh! Four legs good, two legs bad! Moo! Roar! Neeeeigh!'

And with that he disappeared into the bushes.

'HOORAY!' said the crowd, who by this point were just 'HOORAY'-ing any old thing.

'RIGHT,' said the voice in the tree. 'YOU HEARD WHAT OLD HOOF-FEATURES SAID. NOW GET DOWN ON YER KNEES AN' TELL ME WHO'S THE BOSS!'

'Runtus!' said the crowd, falling to their hands and knees.

'WHAT'S THAT? I CAN'T HEAR YOU!'

'Runtus!' chanted the crowd. 'Runtus! Runtus! Runtus!'

'Frides! What we gonna do?' said Polly. 'The

whole town's fallin' for it!'

But Friday O'Leary paid no attention. He was down on his knees with the rest of them, chanting for all he was worth.

'Oh, Frides, you done been tricked as well,' said Polly sadly. 'An' you're usually so sensible.'

'Runtus! Runtus! Runtus!'

The chant grew and grew, like a bad seed that fell into the ground and became an angry sunflower with a gun.

'Runtus! **Runtus!** Runtus!'

It drowned out the birdsong. It drowned out the tinkling of the stream. It drowned out everything, I SAID IT DROWNED OUT EVERYTHING!

'Oh, no!' said Polly. 'Them schoolchildren is at it too! Blow your Teachin' Whistle, Alan Taylor, blow it like a Roman Emp'ror!'

So Alan Taylor blew his Teaching Whistle but of course the chanting drowned it out. And even if they'd heard it the children wouldn't have cared.

'They're turning wild!' sobbed Alan Taylor. 'I hardly know them any more!'

'Come on, A.T., there's nothin' we can do 'bouts it now,' said Polly. 'We better 'scapes before we goes insane.'

And so, Polly and Alan Taylor left that place and no one even bothered to say goodbye. For the folk of Lamonic Bibber were lost – lost to the chants, and the wild ways of the woods.

Chapter 6

Alan Taylor Gets the Pets

'Woe, woe, woe and a bottle of glum,' said Alan Taylor as he and Polly trudged forlornly through the forest, the ground squelching beneath their feet. 'I've lost all my schoolchildren.

I must be the worst headmaster in the world.'

'Don't you be talkin' no nonsenses, you tasty little superstar,' said Polly sympathetically. 'It's not your fault they all runned off like that.'

'Oh, but it is,' wailed Alan Taylor, throwing himself to the forest floor and pounding the earth with his little brown fist. 'I'm a useless teacher! I cZan't do anything right! Even that last sentence I said has got a spelling mistake in it! I'm completely hopeless!'

'Well, what about this little twinkler?' said Polly, pointing to a fuzzy blue caterpillar that was busy licking Alan Taylor's foot. '*He* don't think you're hopeless. He seems to of taken a shine to you.'

'Do you think so?' sniffed Alan Taylor, blowing his nose on a passing stag. 'Do you think I can make him my pet?'

'I don't think you gots any choice,' laughed Polly. 'He's well in love with you.'

'Well, then,' sniffled Alan Taylor. 'I shall call him "Graham". Graham the caterpillar.'

So Polly found some dental floss in her pocket and they made a little lead for Graham. And Alan Taylor cheered up and he looked ever so chirpy walking along with his brand new pet.

'Where are we goin', A.T.?' said Polly as they continued on their way.

'We need to find shelter,' replied Alan Taylor. 'That's the important thing. Then we can –'

But at that moment he happened to glance down, only to see that Graham the caterpillar was holding on to a tiny little lead of his own. At the other end of the lead was a ladybird called Johnny Twospots.

'Why, the little rascal!' laughed Alan Taylor. 'Look, Polly – Graham's found himself a pet too!'

And so they continued through the forest, until they came to a sort of a hollow in the ground.

'What about here for shelter?' said Polly, but Alan Taylor shook his head.

'No,' he said. 'Take a closer look – it's full of wolves.'

So on they went.

'Hey, A.T.!' Polly suddenly exclaimed. 'Johnny Twospots the ladybird done got himself a pet too!' It was an aphid called Penelope. 'Where will it all end?' laughed Polly, who had never seen such fun.

'I don't know,' said Alan Taylor, skip-skappling along, his electric muscles sparking with delight. He was quite back to his usual cheerful self now.

And suddenly the first cuckoo of Spring jumped out from behind a hedge and went

'CUCKOO!' and the first daffodil of Spring jumped out from behind another hedge and went 'DAFFODIL!' and the hedgehogs and the badgers popped up and danced round them three times in a ring and disappeared back into the undergrowth as quickly as they had arrived, and the sun shone down through a gap in the trees and a sparrow sailed past in a little flying birdbath and the entire forest seemed to sparkle with a million million sparkles, one for every single boy and girl in the whole world, even the naughty ones who don't really deserve a sparkle at all.

'Oh, perhaps the forest isn't such a bad place as we done thought!' said Polly, sticking a beautiful wild flower known as a 'Purple Git' in her hair. 'An' with friends an' pets an' giggles-me-gee we won't never lose the day! We'll stop that Runtus madness, we will! I knows it, Alan Taylor, I knows it in my heart!'

'Well spoken, fair nine-year-old maiden of

the forest!' cried Alan Taylor gallantly. 'Now let us away, for methinks shelter is near! Tally-ho, pets, tally-ho!'

The gingerbread petmaster cracked the dental floss – once, twice, three times a lady! And rearing up to their full height, Graham the caterpillar, Johnny Twospots the ladybird and Penelope the aphid led them onwards. Onwards towards the next clearing! Onwards towards shelter! Onwards towards Chapter 7!

Chapter 7

There is no Chapter 7.

Chapter 8

A Plan is Born, and So Are Some Pets

'OK, Polly,' said Alan Taylor, once they were settled in the next clearing. 'We've sorted out shelter – our next challenge is finding something to eat. We must forage for our food, like hunters!' he continued, scrabbling around on the forest floor. 'Look – I've already found a dead bee! And if we're very lucky,' he said hopefully, turning over a small rock . . . 'Yes! Maggots! Now – our next task is to gather sticks to start a fire and –'

'Why don't we jus' go over there?' asked Polly, pointing to a nearby shop:

SQUIRREL McWIRRELL'S GENERAL STORE AND DELICATESSEN
Food, news, tobacco, acorns, etc.

'Oh, yeah,' said Alan Taylor. 'That's a much better idea.'

So off they went to Squirrel McWirrell's shop. (By the way, Squirrel McWirrell wasn't actually a squirrel, that would be crazy. He was a goldfish.)

Five minutes later the heroes were back, stuffing themselves on Cornish pasties, lemonade and sweets, and watching the pets as they capered.

Johnny Twospots was waltzing with a buttercup, Graham the caterpillar was sitting on a mushroom pretending he was in *Alice in Wonderland*, and Penelope the aphid was phoning her mum, who lived in the next forest along.

It was ever so joyful – and yet Polly's heart was heavy as a frankfurter.

'Oh, Alan Taylor,' said Polly. 'I'm well worried 'bout them townsfolk. If it really is Mr Gum up in that cherry tree, then it can't mean no good for no one.'

'Well, that's where I'm one step ahead of you,' winked Alan Taylor, taking one step ahead of her.

'Look what else I bought at Squirrel McWirrell's.'

'A camera!' said Polly. 'But why?'

'Because we need to convince the townsfolk,' said Alan Taylor. 'So if we can get up into that tree ourselves –'

'Then we can do a photograph of him an' we'll have all the proofs we need!' finished Polly. 'Excellent plan, gingerbread man! So how do we –'

But just then the pets came tumbling up.

'Hey,' said Polly. 'Look how fat they all grown, the little greedies!'

It was true. The little pets were no longer all that little.

They were bulgers, one and
all. Graham was a big
fat chubster, Johnny
Twospots   could
hardly even walk
and   Penelope
the aphid was
a b s o l u t e l y
enormous. Well,
for an aphid.

And   then
suddenly:

PLURRRRF!

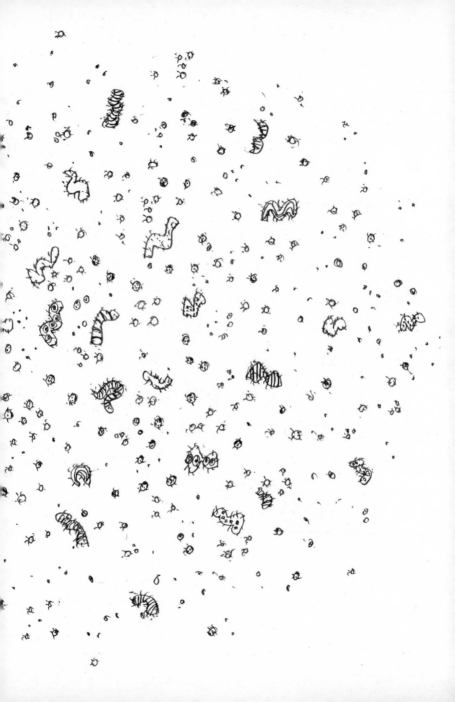

Dozens more pets popped out of them! It was beautiful! But also disgusting!

'EEEEEEUUUUUURGGGH!' cried Polly. 'Alan Taylor! Your pets just done millions of babies all over the place! EEEEUUURGGH!'

'Remarkable,' said Alan Taylor, examining the dozens of new caterpillars, ladybirds and aphids crawling along the forest floor. 'Absolutely remarkable. Come on, Polly. We'd better tether them up.'

So Polly produced the dental floss from her pocket and they spent a happy hour making leads for all the new pets. By the time they were finished, old Mr Twilight was creeping through the forest, turning the day to evening with a flicker of his long goldy fingers. It was that magical hour when anything feels possible, and Polly felt a secret thrill of excitement. *Maybe we was wrong*, she thought as mysterious shadows stretched over the land. *Maybe Runtus really done returned after all . . .*

But there was no time for doubts. The plan was on.

'Right,' said Alan Taylor as he fixed the last lead to a baby caterpillar called Brighton. 'It's time to take a look at that cherry tree.'

Chapter 9

The Dance of the Cherry Tree Goblins

Softly, softly, SOFTLY, SOFTLY, SOFTLY, Polly and Alan Taylor crept through the forest. They'd left the pets behind, being babysat by a kindly old hare.

'Don't worry, I'll look after them,' she hadn't told them. But you knew that's what she was thinking.

So now, here they were, two heroes in the night, creeping towards their destiny and occasionally tripping over small twigs.

'RUNTUS! RUNTUS! RUNTUS!'

The horrible chanting grew louder as Polly and Alan Taylor neared the clearing. And as the last of the day's light flushed away down the toilet of Time, Polly saw a scene that froze the marrow in her bones and turned her blood to ice and turned her hands to snowballs and turned her nose into a carrot and –

'Stop turning into a snowman, Polly,' whispered Alan Taylor. 'We've got important work to do.'

'RUNTUS! RUNTUS! RUNTUS!'

The heroes crept closer.

'RUNTUS! RUNTUS! RUNTUS!'

The heroes crept closer still.

'RUNTUS! RUNTUS! RUNTUS!'

The heroes crept closer than ever.

'RUNTUS! RUNTUS! RUNTUS!'

Alan Taylor's head bashed

into the cherry tree.

'Oops, too close,'

whispered Polly.

The heroes crept

back a bit.

And there they hid, at the edge of the clearing, taking it all in. It was ghastly.

The townsfolk were kneeling in a big circle around the cherry tree, their arms covered with scratches, their hair tangled with leaves and dirt. Their clothes were tattered and torn, and Crazy Barry Fungus's birdcage hadn't been cleaned out all day and smelled so bad that he could hardly breathe.

'What a mess!' whispered Polly. 'They looks like they don't even knows what they're up to!'

'RUNTUS! RUNTUS! RUNTUS!' chanted the crowd.

'RUNTUS! RUNTUS! RU–'

'**SHUT UP!**' roared the voice from the cherry tree suddenly, and at once everyone fell silent. '**I'VE HAD ENOUGH OF YOU FOR ONE DAY! NOW GET LOST! AN' REMEMBER WHAT I TOLD YOU!**'

'Yes, oh great Runtus,' said the townsfolk. 'We have heard your commands. We know what we must do.'

'**TELL ME AGAIN,**' said the voice.

'Tomorrow we must bring you precious gifts,'

chanted the townsfolk. 'We must each bring you the thing that is most precious to us in the whole world.'

'THAT'S RIGHT!' rasped the voice, making the tree rustle from its roots to its leaves. 'NOW PUSH OFF, THE LOT OF YOU! AN' DON'T YOU FORGET THEM GIFTS TOMORROW!'

'We won't, Runtus, we won't!' promised the townsfolk.

'Goodnight, Runtus!' said the little girl called Peter.

'SHUT UP!' snarled Runtus. 'SHABBA ME CHERRY-FILLED WHISKERS! WHAT A BOTHER IT ALL IS.'

'So that's his game,' whispered Polly. 'He jus' wants their riches an' money an' jewels! I might have knowed!'

The heroes watched as the townsfolk

shambled out of the clearing.

'Runtus is the best,' mumbled Jonathan Ripples. 'I can't wait to see him tomorrow.'

'I'm going to give him my most precious gift,' Old Granny muttered to herself. 'Then he'll see how much I love him!'

'THE TRUTH IS A CHERRY TREE MAN!' chanted Friday as he headed off home. 'THE TRUTH IS A CHERRY TREE MAN!'

'That's it, A.T.,' said Polly, hot tears

stinging her cheeks. 'I can't stands to see such shenanigans. We gots to get into that tree rights now!'

'Patience,' cautioned Alan Taylor. 'Let's wait until night's descended on the land like the devil's tablecloth.'

Soon, night descended on the land like the devil's tablecloth.

'That didn't take long,' whispered Alan Taylor, putting on his cheerleader's skirt.

'Now – **One, two!**
One, two, three!
Let's in-vest-i-gate that tree!'

But all of a sudden, the moon came out from behind a cloud, drenching the clearing in its ghostly silver light. And the wind blew as if in answer to the moon, throwing strange bumpy shadows everywhere – and now Polly and Alan Taylor could hear them, cackling, cackling all around.

Creeping out of the bushes. Rustling in the undergrowth. Emerging from rabbit holes.

Busky Pingwood

Yak Triangle

The true horrors of Soupdog

Peeking their dirty little faces out of the shrubs, one by one . . .

'We baccck!' they cackled, and their voices were hard and sharp and cruel. 'We baccckk!'

'Oh, no,' whimpered Alan Taylor, his raisin eyes wide in the moonlight. 'It's the schoolchildren. Only –'

EEK! It's Funk-Whistle

'We baacckk!'
cackled the voices
all around.

'Only they've gone wild again,' he gulped.
'Polly, my schoolchildren
have turned back into
GOBLINS!'

Livermonk

Jingles

Oink Balloon

Dweezil

Captain Ankles

'We baaaa-aaaccck!' cackled the goblins. 'We baaaack!'

Oh, they were back all right! With their teeth and their claws and their extra legs and their tails and their spikes and their horns!

All the old faces were there – Oink Balloon,
Captain Ankles, Livermonk, Soupdog, Mr
Boomerang, Yak Triangle, Wippy . . . And
everyone's favourite –
Big Steve, the big fat
goblin with the
little red hat.

Wippy

Big Steve.
Also: Little
Steve
(under hat)

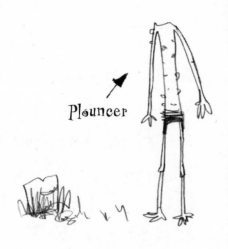

Plouncer

And oh, there were plenty of new ones too, like this tall thin one with no head called Plouncer, and a grubby little belcher called Teenage Loaf who had thirteen arms and a head shaped like a radiator. It was horrible.

Teenage Loaf

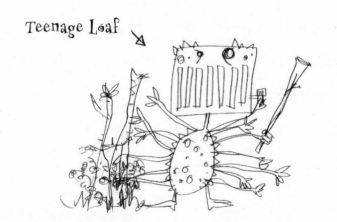

'HA HA HA!' laughed the voice in the cherry tree. 'THAT'S RIGHT! GO WILD, ME FILTHY ARMY OF THE NIGHT!'

And the tree it did rustle and the tree it did shake and the earth it did tremor to see that woeful scene!

'Mussst do sonnng!' squealed Captain Ankles, and at his command the goblins began circling the cherry tree, whooping and hooting and trampling the soil beneath their grubby feet. And Galloping Bill rode out from the bushes, rampant and smelly and untamed 'neath the moonlight, his hooves beating furiously on the wind.

'Cover your ears, Alan Taylor!' cried Polly. 'Cover your ears! They're abouts to do one of their dreadful songs!'

Chapter 10

The Cherry Tree Song*

*featuring a special burp duet from

Livermonk and Teenage Loaf

RUNTUS: I come back from the Olden Days
To sing you all me song!
Up this flippin' cherry tree
A-that's where I belong!

GALLOPING BILL: *An' I'm a brilliant centaur!*
Look at me amazin' hoofs!
Round this cherry tree I'll dance

An' that's the blimmin' truth!

OINK BALLOON: *I wannnt cherrry! Gimmme*
loadds of cherrrries! Me stuffff
them in mouuth an' spit the
stonnnes out on Billl!

GALLOPING BILL: OUCH! OW! NEEIIIGH!
You stupid little squirt!
Stop spitting cherry stones on
me, that one really hurt!

WIPPY: Mee wannnt cherry tooO! Spitt
the stonnnnes on Bill!

SOUPDOG: Mee want cherry tooooOO!!

GALLOPING BILL: OW! OUCH! OW!
OUCH! OUCH! OOOOF!

CHORUS: *Spittt stonnnes on Bill!*
(All the goblins) *Spit stonnnes on BILL!*
Spitt cherrry stonnes on
BIII –IIII -IIIILLL!
Spittt stonnes on BILL!
SPITT STONNES ON BILL!
HA HA! WE GOTT HIM ONN THE
NOSE!

RUNTUS: HA HA HA! Good work, me old goblin army! That's the way to do it! Now, Livermonk! Teenage Loaf! Burp duet! Hit it!

LIVERMONK: BURP!

TEENAGE LOAF: BURP!

LIVERMONK: BURP!

TEENAGE LOAF: BURP! BURP!

LIVERMONK: *BURP!*

TEENAGE LOAF: *BUUUUUUUURP!*

LIVERMONK: *BURP! BURP! BURP!*
BURP! BURP! BURP!
BURP! BURP!

RUNTUS: An' again!

I come back from the Olden Days
To sing you all me rhyme!
Up this flippin' cherry tree
I'm singin' all the time!

LIVERMONK: BURP!

TEENAGE LOAF: BURP!

GALLOPING BILL: OUCH!

OINK BALLOON: CHERRRRRRRIEEEES!
CHERRRRRRIEEES!

RUNTUS: HA HA HA HA HA!

GALLOPING BILL: NEEEIGGGH! OW!

RUNTUS: *Let's do it once again!*

I come back from the Olden Days
To –

'Oh, it's horrible! It's horrible!' moaned Alan Taylor, desperately stuffing bits of grass into his ears.

'I knows!' sobbed Polly. 'They're so out of tune it's unbelievable! I'm tryin' not to listen but it jus' keeps invitin' itself into my head without knockin' first!'

Round the tree the goblins whipped, spitting their cherries and burping their burps and kicking each other in the shins. And Galloping Bill capered around with them, neighing and going 'OW!' quite a lot.

'We gots no chance of gettin' into that tree with all them goblins a-guardin' it!' said Polly. 'They'll mash us up like doorbells!'

But Alan Taylor had another plan.

'Do you see that massive tree, Polly?' he said, pointing to a grand old Duke of a horse chestnut tree, towering above the clearing as if 'twere reaching for the moooooon.

'Yeah,' said Polly. 'It's a right old Conker de la Splonker!'

'Exactly,' said Alan Taylor. 'Now – if we can get up into that horse chestnut, we can shimmy along that branch – do you see – and we can drop into the cherry tree from above. And then we can take our photo and catch Mr Gum in the act!'

'An' them goblins down on the ground won't knows a thing!' exclaimed Polly. 'Alan Taylor, you are the best!'

Chapter 11

An Old Friend Says Hello

*B*URP! BURP! BURP!

Ow! Stop spittin' cherry stones on me!

Ha ha ha! Get 'im, goblins! Pull his tail!

Under cover of the hideous music, Polly and Alan Taylor inched towards the horse chestnut tree. There it stood in the moonlight, towering over the clearing as it had done for hundreds of years, ever since it was just a tiny conker crying in its mother's arms.

'It's a giganter,' said Polly, gazing up at the huge, wide trunk before them. 'How we're ever gonna get up this old belly-boiler I'll never know.'

'Just remember the four Cs,' said little Alan Taylor. 'Climbing, Courage, Confidence and Calling an ambulance after you've fallen out of a horse chestnut tree and broken every single bone in your body.'

Well, the fourth C didn't really fill Polly with much of the third C but there was nothing else to be done. So gathering all her second C, she threw her arms around the trunk and started doing the first C.

'Come on, Polly! You can do it!' urged Alan Taylor as he sat in her hair. 'Yes! That's it! Ooh, you nearly climbed half an inch! Keep going!'

It was no use. The trunk was too wide. Too wide, too steep, too smooth, too slippery, too hundred feet tall.

'I can't do it,' said Polly. 'I can't do it, A.T. It's a' impossible dream. There's jus' no way up an' now we'll never prove who's really in that cherry tree an' the game's lost an' that's the end of that an' I'll has to move to another town where no one knows what a failure I done made, an' I'll open a little shop by the sea what's called **"Lonely Polly's Sea Shells An' Lollipops"**, an' all them lollipops will have sad faces on an' taste bitter as dust an' hardly no one will ever come into my shop an' there I'll sit all day long, sighin' an' lookin' out the window over the rainy beach, lookin' out to sea an' thinkin' 'bout a little place called Lamonic Bibber what I once did love.'

And with that, poor Polly slumped against the tree and began to sob. Alan Taylor offered his hanky but it was only the size of a postage stamp, just enough for one teardrop and no more.

But Lo! Lo! Lo! Whatever that means.

Just when all seemed lost there came a bark. Not a tree bark – there was already plenty of that, that was the problem – but a bark such as the noise what occasionally emerges out of the mouths of dogs.

'Look up, Polly!' cried Alan Taylor, his raisin eyes agleam.

And yes, the astonishing truth was that an enormous Jupiter of a dog was bounding down the tree trunk towards them, a massive WHOPPER of a dog in fact, and what? No! Really? Seriously? YES! It was none other than that magnificent beasterliser –

'JAKE!' shouted Polly as the huge golden furhound flamped it down the tree, barking it up like a chostril and singing his song of old:

Bark bark bark
Bark
Baaaaaaaaaaark
Bark bark bark bark
Bark bark
Woof

It was amazing but true. Polly and Alan Taylor had stumbled across the one and only secret and legendary horse chestnut tree in which Jake the dog lived.

'Oh, Jakey! Jakey!' said Polly, throwing her arms around that good boy's back and hugging him 'til he dribbled. 'So this is where you calls home! An' now you can takes us up to your nest and we can do our plan and the townsfolk won't be fooled no more an' I won't haves to live by the sea bein' sad! Oh, you lovely, lovely, lovely, lovely, lovely, *lovely* woofdog!'

In an instant the heroes had hopped on to Jake's broad back and he was zipping up the tree trunk like he didn't even care. His famous claws dug into the bark! His famous tail swung like the rudder of a great ship, steering him straight and true! His not-quite-so-famous knees did whatever it is that dog's knees do! It was remarkable and that is why I remarked on it!

Oh, if you haven't ever gone scrambling up a horse chestnut tree on the back of a massive whopper of a dog in the middle of the night, you haven't lived, my friends! The air riffled through their hair, the owls and the pipistrelles flurried and how Polly wished the ride could last forever! But nothing lasts forever, not even school assembly, although it sometimes feels like it.

All too soon the heroes were standing

high up in Jake's nest amongst his collection of broken radios, old magazines and paperclips he had found lying in the forest.

'What a clever woof-crumble you is, Jake!' said Polly, stroking his big soft belly. 'You done made your home in 'xactly the right place to help us investigates that cherry tree!'

'WOOF,' said Jake, who didn't really know what was going on.

Polly sat on the edge of the branch and

looked down. The little cherry tree was a long way below her dangling legs. The goblins were just dark dots in the distance. And Galloping Bill was just a dark dot being hit by cherry stones.

Now Polly was up here it didn't seem quite so easy. It was far too long a way to jump down into the tree. There was only one thing for it . . .

Polly doubled a long strand of dental floss around the branch.

'Be careful,' said Alan Taylor solemnly.

'BARK!' said Jake.

'BURP!' said Livermonk, far below.

The song had finally ended.

And then the night was silent. The moon blinked once, then looked away. Somewhere in the distance nothing happened.

Polly took a deep breath. Then she slid off the branch, gripping the dental floss for her very life.

Down she went, through the dark unseeing night.

Heading for the cherry tree.

Heading for Runtus.

Chapter 12

In the Cherry Tree

Down went Polly into the cherry tree. Down she slid through the dark green leaves. Down, down into the very heart of the tree, where the secrets lay. And suddenly she was scared. What if it really *was* Runtus? What if she was about to meet an ancient woodland spirit, a spirit with horns on his head and the legs of a goat and a magic flute so powerful that one note from it could stop the world from turning, or blow up a koala? Shaking like a leaf, Polly pushed aside the shaking leaves. And there she saw him.

Yes, there he was, sitting astride a branch and swigging from a bottle of –

GALLOPING BILL'S
HOMEMADE
FOREST CIDER

INGREDIENTS: Cherries, entrails,
beer, bit of an old shoe, couple of
spiders, somethin' I found in me ear,
acorns, magpie beak, fresh lemon
juice (not from concentrate)
Counts as two of your recommended
five spiders a day

WARNING: May cause headaches and mild death

It was Mr Gum. His big red scruffler of a beard dripped with cherry juice. His hands were as filthy as pubs. And his bloodshot eyes were lit up with madness and power.

'I knews it!' said Polly. 'I knews it was you all along! An' I bet Gallopin' Bill isn't nothin' but that stinker of a butcher, Billy William the Third!'

'It's true!' cried Galloping Bill gleefully, poking his dirty face up through the leaves. 'I made this costume meself, from a dead horse!

Neeeeigggh!' he boasted, before disappearing into the night once more.

'Well, you annoyin' little frog,' said Mr Gum, turning to Polly with a snarl. 'You was right about Billy an' you was right about me. Satisfied?'

'Not yet,' said Polly bravely. 'You see, I'm here to get proofers that there isn't no Runtus after all.'

And with that she whipped out the camera and aimed it at Mr Gum's crooked face. But before she could click the shutter, Billy popped his head back up through the leaves, opened his mouth as wide as he could and swallowed the camera whole.

'HA HA HA! Good one, Billy, me old centaur-impersonator!' laughed Mr Gum. 'Oh, deary me,' he sneered, turning back to Polly. 'You got no proof an' you never will! How are them townsfolk gonna believe you now, you pathetic flea?'

'I got my word!' said Polly. 'That's what!'

'Your word?' snorted Mr Gum, laughing so hard that a cherry stone shot out of his nostril.

'Your WORD? It's me them townsfolk listen to these days, so move over, little girl! There's a new little girl in town – me!'

'But why?' pleaded Polly. 'Why are you doin' this terrible thing?'

'Cos I fancies RULIN' this stupid forest!' laughed Mr Gum, his bloodshot eyes lighting up with a terrible greed so greedy it was very greedy indeedy. 'An' not only that but I'm gonna rule the whole stupid TOWN of Lamonic Bibber too!

AN' RULE 'EM I WILL!' he roared, so loudly that the branches shook and the leaves trembled and a load of cider bottles plummeted out of the tree, smashing their glassy way through the night.

'OW!' said Billy from below.

'That's right,' said Mr Gum. 'I'm gonna rule this town. I'm already half way there. An' tomorrow's the big day.'

'What's so important 'bout tomorrow?' said Polly.

Mr Gum danced on the branch in his hobnail boots, his face half in shadow, half in light like a swine who didn't know better.

'I ain't tellin' you!' he laughed, cracking open another bottle of cider. 'Now get out of me tree 'fore I kick you out with me fists! Now get out of me tree 'fore I –'

Well, Polly didn't need telling twice. Hastily she climbed down from the tree and ran off into the night, the goblins' cackling calls chasing her through the darkness.

'Neeeeigh!' cried Billy as he watched her go.
'Neeeeigggh! Neeeeiggh! Neeeigggh! Neeeiggh!
Neeeeiggh! Neeeeigghh! Neeei –'

'Shut it, Billy,' growled Mr Gum, who wanted
nothing more than to snooze the rest of the night
away in peace. 'Yer not actually a real centaur,
you idiot.'

'But I like doin' it!' laughed Billy. 'It's funty!
Neeeeigh! Neeeigh! Neeeigh! Neiggh! Neeiiiiigh!

Neeeiggh! Neeiiigh! Neeiiigh! Neeeigh!'

'BURP!' went Livermonk.

'Neeeiiigh!' went Billy.

'WOOF!' joined in Jake from above. 'WOOF WOOF WOOFITY WOOF WOOF WOOF!'

'I'm surrounded by idiots,' sighed Mr Gum, shaking his head in despair. 'Sometimes I dunno why I even bother, I really don't.'

Chapter 13

Babies and Rainbows

*O*h, how the gingerbread headmaster and his pets rejoiced upon Polly's return! Alan Taylor beamed, Graham the caterpillar purred with pleasure and Johnny Twospots danced a new ballet called *The Return of Polly* in her honour. But Penelope the aphid just sulked in the corner, for secretly, deep down in her aphid heart, she was jealous of Polly's friendship with Alan Taylor. You see, aphids are very jealous creatures and that is why they are green.

'Oh, Alan Taylor,' said Polly, 'I been into the cherry tree an' just you guess what? We was right! It wasn't nothin' but Mr Gum business in there, plain an' simple. Only I didn't get no photo cos Billy William done scoffed my camera an' – EEEEUUURGGH! Your pets is doin' millions more babies!'

PLUUUURF!

PLUUUUURF!

It was true. The pets were squeezin' an' a-sneezin' new babies out all over the place. And not just the old pets, either. Lots of the younger ones were at it too, popping 'em out like jinstrels.

PLLLLUUUUURRRF!

'Remarkable,' said Alan Taylor, examining the many new scuttlers. 'They never seem to stop! Come on, Polly – we've lots of new leads to make!'

But the night's adventures had been too much. Polly had already fallen into a lovely deep sleep where there were no cherry trees and no goblins and no Runtuses trying to rule the town. Just lovely fluffy clouds which rained strawberry lemonade, and a big fairytale castle filled with tall handsome princes who all looked like Jake with a moustache.

When Polly awoke, dawn was breaking overhead. The sun was brushing its shiny blonde hair, the trees were stretching their backs and the birds were singing their latest hit, '**CHIRP CHIRP CHIRP** (2010 Maximum Funk remix)'. The day was going to be a beauty. A little way off, Alan Taylor sat in the dewy grass, watching his hundreds of pets play and tumble around. He looked so happy sitting there that Polly couldn't help but feel her spirits rise.

And talking of spirits . . .

'How I do love the forest at this time of day,' said a voice at Polly's side. 'It reminds me of when the world was young and smelled of hope and roses.'

Polly turned to look – and there beside her was the Spirit of the Rainbow, his honest face sparkling in the dewdrop morning light. Just looking at him filled Polly with marvellous feelings, as if she was somehow a forest herself, full of wonderful flowers and streams, and suddenly she knew – he had come to teach her lessons and ancient wisdoms or something.

'Child,' said the Spirit of the Rainbow, though he was no older than she. 'I remember this forest many hundreds of years ago. It was a wild, carefree place. Can you guess how many chocolate wrappers and other bits of litter there were mucking it up?'

'Six?' said Polly.

'None,' came the lad's astonishing answer. 'None at all. You see, child, the world was full of wonder back then. There were fauns and centaurs – yes, *actual real* centaurs. One of them was called Tony. And there were pixies and elves and wood nymphs. And there were transparent sprites with almond-shaped eyes, bathing in every stream. It was excellent.'

'Was there unicorns too?' asked Polly, who had always wanted more than anything to find a unicorn and ride it to the moon.

'No, there never were any unicorns,' said the lad. 'That was just a myth that started when an ice-cream cone accidentally got stuck to a pony's head.'

'Oh,' said Polly. But she could not stay disappointed for long, not with the sun dappling through the treetops and the smell of fresh pine and wooded oak, and the Spirit of the Rainbow's face, as he remembered those far-off times when things were simple and free.

'Yes, free,' said the Spirit of the Rainbow. 'Look at Alan Taylor, child, for this is the lesson I want to share.'

Polly looked over at the gingerbread headmaster. He was laughing in the grass, pets bouncing up and down on him – caterpillars, ladybirds and aphids! Caterpillars, ladybirds and aphids! Bouncy, bouncy, bouncy! It was tremendous.

'See how he lets his pets go free,' observed

the Spirit of the Rainbow.

'Yes,' said Polly. 'He loves walkin' them on their leads – but he's always givin' 'em time off to have their fun when they needs it.'

'How right he is,' said the lad. 'But there is someone in this forest who NEVER lets anyone go free.'

'Yes,' shuddered Polly. 'Mr Gum.'

'Exactly,' said the lad. 'Mr Gum is like a cruel pet-owner who wants his pets to be tied up all the time. Only Mr Gum's pets are not caterpillars or insects –'

'They're the townsfolk!' finished Polly. 'He's treatin' the townsfolk jus' like he owns 'em.'

'Yes, child,' said the Spirit of the Rainbow sombrely. 'He is promising everyone they will be free, but really he's just trying to control them.'

'So what you're sayin' is –'

'What I am saying, child, is not what is important,' said the boy. 'For words are merely words. And sounds are merely sounds. And once every hundred years a flower with the face of an angel blooms in a white tower and cries tears of pure love. But enough of these mysteries! Time draws on and I must away. I've got a swimming lesson at ten-thirty.'

'But jus' tell me one thing,' said Polly as the boy got up to go. 'Was Runtus ever real? Back when the forests was excellent with all them pixies an' fairies an' sprites – was Runtus there too?'

For a moment it seemed the boy would tell her. His mouth opened – but then he seemed to think better of it.

'I must away,' he said, disappearing into the dazzling sunshine. And where he had sat were three fruit chews. One said 'YES', one said 'NO' and one said 'MAYBE'.

Chapter 14

Precious Things

'*R*UNTUS! RUNTUS! RUNTUS!'

The sun was climbing higher through the treetops as one by one the townsfolk returned to the clearing. Old Granny, Jonathan Ripples, Martin Launderette, The Pamelas, the other Pamela who no one liked, Crazy Barry

Fungus and many others besides. And they all
had one thing in common: they all had faces.
And they all had another thing in common: each
and every one of them was carrying a gift for
Runtus.

Jonathan Ripples was carrying a photo of
himself as a young man, thin and handsome like
a film star, all those years before the hunger had
got him.

'RUNTUS! RUNTUS! RUNTUS!'

Martin Launderette had brought the toy washing machine he'd played with as a child. How he'd love to fill it with toy shirts and toy trousers and toy washing powder that was actually sherbet! And it was that toy washing machine that had made him want to open a launderette when he grew up.

'RUNTUS! RUNTUS! RUNTUS!'

Beany McLeany, who loved things that
rhymed, had brought his
favourite things of all:
a   stuffed   raccoon,
a tablespoon and a
blue balloon.
'RUNTUS!
RUNTUS!!'

Friday O'Leary had brought a photo taken on his wedding day. The photo was actually of a doorknob factory in Liverpool but never mind. It had been taken on his wedding day and that was the important thing.

'I don't get it,' said Alan Taylor, from where he and Polly lay hidden behind a tulip, the pets grazing at their side. 'This stuff's just worthless junk. What on earth can Mr Gum want with it?'

'I dunno,' said Polly slowly. 'I thought he was after their riches. But –'

She looked at the townsfolk again. Seeing the dreamy way they gazed at their precious things. Seeing the careful way they held them . . .

Suddenly she understood it all, and a chill went up her spine and a caterpillar went down her sock.

'That's it!' cried Polly. 'These *are* precious things, A.T.! They're precious in the hearts of them townsfolks! They're the things what gives 'em hope an' reminds 'em of happier times.'

'You're right!' exclaimed Alan Taylor. 'By ginger, you're right, Polly!'

'An' if they gives 'em up, it's like they're givin'

up a part of themselves!' continued Polly. 'It's GAME OVER an' Mr Gum'll have total control of 'em all, just like he done planned! They'll be at his command forever!'

'Oh, Polly!' cried Alan Taylor. 'He's not just taking their precious things – it's like he's stealing their very SOULS!'

Polly gritted her teeth.

'Well, he hasn't got 'em yet,' she said determinedly. 'We gotta stop him before it's too late. It's no use stopping him *after* it's too late cos it'll be too late!'

'Well, come on then,' said Alan Taylor gallantly. 'Tally-ho, pets, tally-ho!'

And so they followed the crowd into the clearing, brave Polly and little Alan Taylor and his hundreds of pets all rearing up before him like a vast, moving sea of blue and yellow and green.

'RUNTUS! RUNTUS! RUNTUS!'

The townsfolk encircled the tree, waving their precious things.

'RUNTUS! RUNTUS! RUNTUS!'

'Oh, great Runtus, we have brought you our precious gifts just as you asked! For you are our mighty leader and –'

'OI, TOWNSFOLK!' shouted Polly, racing

into their midst. 'Shut up with all your "RUNTUS"es an' listen, cos I gots news so astoundin' that your minds is gonna explode out your faces an' your legs is gonna melt with astonishment an' your arms is gonna fly out their sockets an' land on a nearby hill!'

'You'd better not tell us then,' said David Casserole, the Mayor. 'That sounds absolutely horrible.'

'No, you gots to know,' said Polly. 'Cos you all

been taken for fools by that cherry tree. Cos now I know for sure – it isn't no Runtus up in them leaves. No! It's Mr Gum! I seen him myself, hidin' there like a dirty great maggot with a hat on!'

'What?!' murmured the crowd. 'Not Runtus? Hmm! Murmur! Murmur! Hmm! Murmur! Hmm! Debate! Murmur! Murmur!'

'Hang on,' demanded Martin Launderette, suddenly turning on Polly. 'Why should we take *your* word for it?'

'Yes,' cried Jonathan Ripples. 'Where's your proof?'

'I haven't got none,' admitted Polly. 'Unfortunately my camera was eaten by a pretend centaur. But –'

'No buts!' declared Mayor Casserole. 'It's Runtus we like and it's Runtus we came to see. Sorry, Polly, but the Old Ways are back and they're here to stay!'

Chapter 15

Runtus and the Pets

'*R*UNTUS! RUNTUS! RUNTUS!'

The noise was deafening. It was so awful that the bluebells pressed their emergency REWIND buttons and shot back underground. It was so horrible that the weeping willows wept real tears. It was so unbearable that the elm trees elmigrated to another country.

'RUNTUS! RUNTUS! RUNTUS!' chanted the crowd. And then there came the most almighty cheer as Galloping Bill stepped out from the bushes, the gang of grinning goblins at his side.

'Neeeeigh! Neeeeigh!' said Galloping Bill, pawing at the morning air like he imagined a real centaur might do. 'Now, I know you all come here to see yer favourite woodlan' spirit! Am I right?'

'YES!' yelled the crowd.

'Neeeeigh! Miaow! Who do you wanna see?' shouted Galloping Bill, in his centaur-iest voice yet.

'RUNTUS!' yelled the crowd.

'Well then, yer in luck!' cried Galloping Bill, accidentally punching himself in the face with excitement. 'Cos here comes the bloke what you loves to obey! The one what's got important commands to say! The one what's gonna change your lives today! It's the one . . . the only . . . RUNTUS! Neeeeeeiggggghhh!'

'YEAH!' shouted the voice in the cherry tree as the crowd roared. 'THAT'S RIGHT, ME OLD DEVOTED FOLLOWERS! IT'S ME! NOW, YOU ALL GOT YER PRECIOUS GIFTS TO SHOW HOW MUCH YOU LOVE ME?'

'Yes!' shouted the crowd.

'GOOD. NOW HERE'S HOW IT'S GONNA

WORK! YOU GOTTA GO OVER TO GALLOPIN'
BILL AN' GIVE HIM YER PRECIOUS THINGS!
IT'S AS SIMPLE AS A, B, RUNTUS! SO – WHO'S
GONNA GO FIRST?'

'Old Granny should go first,' shouted
someone. 'She's the one who led us here.'

'Yes, Old Granny should go first!' shouted
someone else.

'Yes, Old Granny!' shouted someone else.

'I don't think Old Granny should go first!'

shouted someone else. But they were overruled. It was democracy.

Trembling like a croissant, Old Granny started forward. And the goblins taunted her as she went, gobbing cherry stones and pulling bad faces.

'Stuppppid oldd womman!' cackled Captain Ankles.

'Look, she gott rubbbbish unfashionable hairrstyle!' said Oink Balloon. 'Ha ha ha!'

And now Old Granny was kneeling in front of Galloping Bill.

'Here,' she whispered, handing him a piece of paper. It was ancient and yellow at the edges, and it was barely hanging together. It was a love letter from her first husband, written the day he'd been shipped off to the War:

Dear Old Granny

I'm afraid they're shipping me off
to the War. Who? I do not know. Why?
I do not know. What War? I have no
idea. But of one thing I am certain
- I love your face and everything
underneath it. I love all of you, Old
Granny, and that is why I married
you. You are the best.

Adieu, my love
Your adoring husband

Old Manny

Xx

P.S. - Don't touch the sherry I left
in the drinks cabinet.

'Is that yer most precious possession in the whole stupid world?' sneered Galloping Bill.

'It is,' said Old Granny.

'Then hand it over,' he demanded.

For a moment Old Granny seemed about to refuse. But then she bowed her head and handed it over. And as the letter left her hand, something in Old Granny's eyes seemed to flash once, and then die out altogether.

'Got it!' shouted Galloping Bill triumphantly.

'NICE ONE,' rasped Runtus. 'NOW, OLD GRANNY. REPEAT AFTER ME: "I HAVE GIVEN UP ME MOST PRECIOUS POSSESSION."'

'I have given up my most precious possession,' repeated Old Granny.

'"AN' NOW I WILL DO ANYTHIN' FOR RUNTUS,"' said the voice.

'And now I will do anything for Runtus,' said Old Granny.

'"ME SOUL BELONGS TO RUNTUS

FOREVER!'" said the voice.

'My soul –' began Old Granny, her voice trembling.

The crowd cheered. The goblins cackled.

'My soul,' croaked Old Granny, through lips as dry as sand. 'My soul belongs to –'

But suddenly it hit Polly like a multi-coloured bolt of lightning thrown into her brain by Cleveros, the God of Brilliant Ideas. Without a moment's thought she snatched the lead from

Alan Taylor's gingerbread hand.

'Polly!' he cried in shock. 'What are you up to?'

'Sorry, A.T.,' she replied, 'but I jus' thought of somethin' the Spirit of the Rainbow done told me. Mr Gum's controllin' everyone like pets on leads. But sometimes you gots to let them pets go FREE!'

Polly bit through the dental floss – and the pets were off the lead.

For a moment they just stood there doing nothing. A few of them popped out some last-minute babies. Then a great gust of wind picked them up and in that gust of wind Polly thought – just for a moment – that she could hear the Spirit of the Rainbow's voice.

'Go freeeeeee, little ones,' it seemed to say. 'Go freeeee!'

The gust of wind blew the pets towards the cherry tree.

Caterpillars, ladybirds, aphids. Hundreds of them. Thousands of the little tanglers. They landed in the lovely green leaves of the tree.

And . . .

It was one of the biggest nibbles the world had ever heard.

In China people looked up at the noise and said, 'Hmm, sounds like some caterpillars and ladybirds are nibbling a cherry tree over in England. Oh, and maybe some aphids too.'

In Egypt the nibbling sound took a famous prince by surprise, causing him to trip over a prune.

In San Francisco a team of Nibbleologists measured the nibble at 48.4 on the Official Nibble Scale. 'It's astounding!' said the Chief Nibbleologist. 'Especially as the Official Nibble Scale only goes up to 12. And especially as there's no such thing as Nibbleologists in the first place.'

Yes, it was a nibble of outstanding proportions, The Nibble That Shook The World.

And then it was over. The caterpillars floated gently to earth on little parachutes of silk. And the ladybirds flew down with them, and the aphids hitch-hiked on their spotty backs. But the townsfolk hardly noticed, for they were gazing at the cherry tree in shock.

The pets had feasted well. They'd stripped every single leaf from the cherry tree. Every last one. And now the Lord of the Cherry Tree was revealed in all his filthy glory.

Caught in the bare branches of the tree like the guiltiest spatula imaginable.

'Well, townsfolk,' said Polly quietly. 'There's your "Runtus". There's the one you was about to give your souls to, you sillies.'

And the townsfolk saw they'd been played for fools by a master scoundrel.

There was the briefest of pauses. Then –

'GET HIMMMMMM!'

Jonathan Ripples flew at the tree trunk, battering it with his bulk.

KA-FLING!

Mr Gum was knocked clear out of the branches.

KA-FLY-THROUGH-THE-AIR!

Mr Gum flew through the air.

KA-LAND-JUST-TO-THE-SIDE-OF-BILLY!

Not really. Mr Gum landed right on top of Billy, splattering him up like a squirtflake.

'GET 'EM!' roared the crowd.

'SHABBA ME LYIN', DECEIVIN' WHISKERS!' shouted Mr Gum. 'They'll rip us to shreds an' put each shred in a different prison! Come on, Billy me boy, gimme a ride out of here!'

And like the coward he was, Mr Gum clambered on to Billy's back and together they snoofed it out that forest just as fast as you please, or maybe even faster.

'GET BACK HERE!' roared the crowd. 'WE HAVEN'T FINISHED WITH YOU!' But though the townsfolk chased those villains for the rest of that day, somehow they managed to escape. For never was there a pair of rascals more slippery than Mr Gum and Billy William the Third, and that is why they are sometimes given the nickname 'The Pair of Slippers'. And just like slippers they were gone, gone, gone. Gone where the wind would carry 'em. Gone where the wind would blow.

Chapter 16

Feasts and Such

So that's how the townsfolk's souls were saved. And with the danger over it was time for a feast. The children ran hither and thither, picking wise berries from the trees, and Old Granny tested the berries to see if they were poisonous by asking each and every one, 'Are you poisonous?' The little girl called Peter made daisy chains to hang from the branches, and the little boy called Rita made daisy padlocks to make sure no one stole them. Jonathan Ripples went out bravely hunting and returned with wild boar and rabbits, and Martin Launderette pretended he'd caught them himself and Jonathan Ripples sat on him to teach him a lesson.

And Friday O'Leary played the drums with

a rat-and-a-tat-and-a-wiggle-of-his-hat, and then what do you think? Jake the dog came bounding down from his horse chestnut tree and it was time for stroking and patting and riding round on his great broad furry back. Broad as a beam it was, broad as a beam!

And as the evening drew on, a bonfire was lit in the clearing and the food and wine flowed freely, my friends. And everywhere that Polly looked she saw the townsfolk, not as they had been when they were under Mr Gum's spell but as they should be, merry and bright-eyed and sometimes a bit drunk, especially Old Granny. And the goblins turned back into children and said sorry and Alan Taylor forgave them. And then the caterpillars all got together and did a load of cocoons and on the stroke of midnight – **PLIM!** – they turned into butterflies.

'Goodbye, little friends,' said Alan Taylor as the creatures flapped out of the forest, but it wasn't goodbye – for all summer long those butterflies were seen flying through Lamonic Bibber, cheering people up with their colourful wings and sometimes being eaten by cats or getting stuck in electric fans.

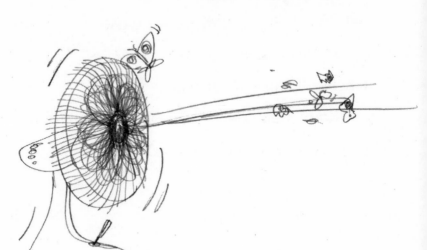

And as for Polly and her friends – Friday O'Leary, little Alan Taylor and big slobbery Jake – well, they'd never been happier.

'I wonder if there ever *was* a real Runtus in these parts,' said Polly as they cleared up after the feast. 'What does you think, everyone?'

'Hmm,' said Friday O'Leary, gazing thoughtfully into the distance.

'Hmm,' said Alan Taylor, gazing thoughtfully into the distance, only lower.

'WOOF!' said Jake, nuzzling Penelope the aphid. They had become quite good friends.

Suddenly remembering something, Polly reached into her skirt pocket and pulled out the three fruit chews the Spirit of the Rainbow had given her. She handed one to each of her companions.

'So,' she asked again. 'Does you think Runtus was ever real?'

'YES,' said Friday, reading what was written on his sweet wrapper.

'NO,' said Alan Taylor, reading what was written on his.

Polly looked down at the wrapper of her own fruit chew. 'MAYBE,' she said. 'Maybe.'

And they all stood there in the grove, gazing at the cherry tree as dusk drew in, chewing it over.

THE END

EPILOGUE

It is the early hours before dawn and the forest clearing stands empty and still. All the people have long since gone home, and aside from an owl arguing with a badger about whether or not squirrels can talk, the grove is silent, bathed in magical, heavenly moonlight.

But now – what's this? A tapping can be heard, a tip-tapping from across the way. And over the burbling crystal blue stream, comes a rider on a horse. No, not a rider on a horse at all! But a strange creature with the body of a fine strong stallion and the chest and head of a handsome young man.

'Oh, great one,' says he, clip-clopping over to the cherry tree which stands tall and graceful in the centre of the clearing. 'It is safe now. They have all gone.'

'Are you sure?' says a voice – and now a small figure can be seen climbing out from inside of the tree trunk itself. A figure with a flute and curly hair, and the shaggy legs of a goat. 'Are you quite sure they have gone, Tony?'

'Yes, great Runtus,' says Tony the Centaur. 'Those crazy humans are gone at last. And now we can play.'

Then Runtus puts the flute to his lips and plays three quick notes – one, two, three. And from far and near the creatures of the Olden Days come bounding and skipping into the grove. Fauns, leprechauns, those sprites with their almond-shaped eyes . . . It's all happening. Elves, fairies, all sorts of wild creatures. And finally, trotting into the clearing, the very last guest of the party – a beautiful unicorn, with a horn of pure gold on his forehead and moon dust on his hooves.

'See, Tony?' laughs Runtus, as he skips and capers with his friends through the woodlands that he loves. 'There <u>are</u> real unicorns after all. That Spirit of the Rainbow doesn't know everything!'

FIN

Hey, kids!

Ever heard of Turkey the flag popper? I have! Want to know more? Then read on. Don't want to know more? Then don't read on. Want to throw bacon into the sea? Then for goodness' sake throw bacon into the sea, no one's stopping you.

Anyway. Here it is, whether you like it or not . . .

Turkey the
Flag Popper

'YES!' cried Friday O'Leary excitedly, waving his newspaper frantically up and down. 'I knew it! I knew he'd come!'

'Who?' cried everyone.

'Turkey!' shouted Friday. 'Turkey the flag popper!'

'Who's he?' cried Polly.

'What's he do?' squeaked Alan Taylor.

'Where's he from?' shouted Old Granny.

'Who does his laundry?' yelled Martin Launderette.

'Why, don't you know? Don't you see? Don't you even understand?' shouted Friday, producing his trumpet and piano from his top pocket. 'It's Turkey! Turkey the flag popper!'

Don't you know? Don't you see?
Don't you even understand?
He's got a great big orange
and he holds it in his hand!
And he roams the highways
and the byways up and down this land
Turkey the flag popper!

He's always in a rush except he's
sometimes in a bush
And he puts a lot of gravy in his tea
He's got a great big pencil
and it sits behind his ear!
He's not round when you need him
– when you don't he's always near
I saw him eat a ladder once,
but why, it was not clear
Turkey the flag popper!

In the mornings he always
phones his mother!
In the afternoons he always
phones his brother!
In the evenings he phones
someone or other!
In the night time he always
phones his mother
again.

Have you seen him?
Do you hear him?
For he's coming up the path
He's taller than a kestrel and
he likes a long hot bath
He's got a great big chocolate cake,
it's balanced on his head
I saw him eat a crayon once
– the crayon it was red
And when he'd scoffed it
down, my word, it turned
HIM red instead
Turkey the flag popper!

Do you know just where he gets to
In the middle of the night?
When all the wigwam
children are asleep?
He climbs upon a tennis ball
And rolls across the waves
And he plays with all the
monsters of the deep!

I've seen him in America
I've seen him in the East
I've seen him knitting
underwear for bees!
He's got a great big piece of stone
he carries round and round
He stole it from a building
in an old Italian town
And that is why the Leaning
Tower of Pisa's falling down
Turkey the flag popper!

Don't you know?
Can't you tell?
Don't you even have a clue?
He's ninety per cent water
and the rest of him is glue!
His best friend was a crocodile
but now he's just a shoe!
Turkey the flag popper!
Yes, Turkey the flag popper!
Yes, it's Turkey the fla-a-a-g popper!

'We gots to go an' see him!' said Polly when the song was done and Friday was slumped in his favourite armchair, trying to get his breath back. 'Oh, Friday, lets!'

☆ ☆ ☆

So that night they all camped out in the Old Meadow, waiting for Turkey the flag popper to appear. But he never did.

'Well,' said Friday in satisfaction. 'Not even bothering to turn up – that's just like old Turkey. What a rascal he is!'

THE END

About the Author

Andy Stanton lives in North London. He studied English at Oxford but they kicked him out. He has been a film script reader, a cartoonist, an NHS lackey and lots of other things. He has many interests, but best of all he likes cartoons, books and music (even jazz). One day he'd like to live in New York or Berlin or one of those places because he's got fantasies of bohemia. His favourite expression is 'I like straws' and his favourite word is 'upstart'. This is his seventh book.

About the Illustrator

David Tazzyman lives in South London with his girlfriend, Melanie, and their son, Stanley. He grew up in Leicester, studied illustration at Manchester Metropolitan University and then travelled around Asia for three years before moving to London in 1997. He likes football, cricket, biscuits, music and drawing. He still dislikes celery.

www.mrgum.co.uk

You've read the book, now visit the 82% official
Mr Gum website at: www.mrgum.co.uk
It's full to bursting with things like:

- AN EPISODE OF THE ALBTA award-winning
  ## 'Bag of Sticks'

- BUTCHER'S DARTS!

- BOOK INFORMATION AND NEWS!

- PHOTOS!

- *Ask Andy:* A chance to submit your very own
  question to Mr Andy Stanton!

- ## The Lamonical Chronicle
  (see over for more details)

In fact, there are so many things on the website we can't
even be bothered trying to fit them all on this page.

Read All About it!

The Lamonical Chronicle

Visit www.mrgum.co.uk to subscribe to Lamonic Bibber's second best, & only, newspaper.

It's free! And you can win prizes!

Huzzah!

HEY, JONAH!

How much fun is the audio version of

'You're A Bad Man, Mr Gum!'?

HA HA HA! HA! HA! HAHAHAHHA!
CHORTLE! SNICKER! HA HA! ERK!
HA! OOP! HA HA AH AHA! HA! HA!
HA HA HA! EEP! NORP!
HAHAHAHAHAHA!
HA HA!

HA HA
HA HA
EEEP!

SNORTLE!

Yes, Jonah is exactly 100% correct. The 'Mr Gum' audiobook thingy is so funny you won't be able to speak, maybe forever. And guess who reads it? Me! And guess who I am? Andy Stanton! So get it today, you nibbleheads – it's like reading a book with your ears!

Available on CD, over the internet, by phone or inside the bellies of magic frogs. To order a copy or for more information go to www.bbcshop.com or phone 01225 443400.

(Headphones not supplied. But maybe you can borrow a spare pair off Jonah, he seems to have far too many.)

EGMONT PRESS: ETHICAL PUBLISHING

Egmont Press is about turning writers into successful authors and children into passionate readers – producing books that enrich and entertain. As a responsible children's publisher, we go even further, considering the world in which our consumers are growing up.

Safety First
Naturally, all of our books meet legal safety requirements. But we go further than this; every book with play value is tested to the highest standards – if it fails, it's back to the drawing-board.

Made Fairly
We are working to ensure that the workers involved in our supply chain – the people that make our books – are treated with fairness and respect.

Responsible Forestry
We are committed to ensuring all our papers come from environmentally and socially responsible forest sources.

For more information, please visit our website at www.egmont.co.uk/ethical

---

Egmont is passionate about helping to preserve the world's remaining ancient forests. We only use paper from legal and sustainable forest sources, so we know where every single tree comes from that goes into every paper that makes up every book.

This book is made from paper certified by the Forestry Stewardship Council (FSC), an organisation dedicated to promoting responsible management of forest resources. For more information on the FSC, please visit **www.fsc.org**. To learn more about Egmont's sustainable paper policy, please visit **www.egmont.co.uk/ethical**.

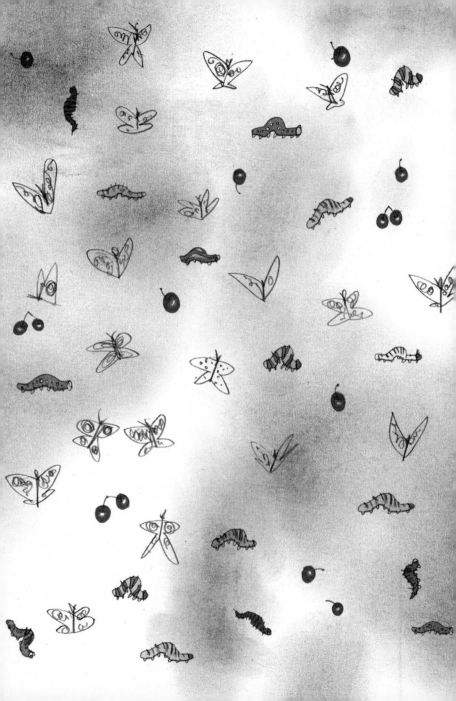

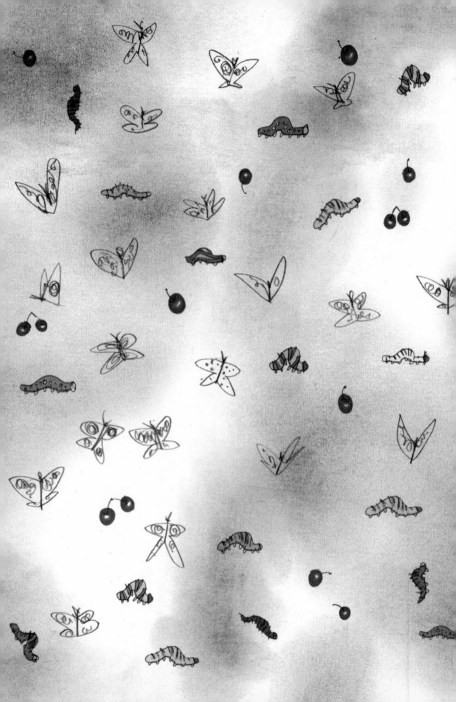